On One Foot

To Michaela Shamblott, with appreciation and affection—for all
the years and all the fun we had in Room 1. —L.G.

To all artists who fill this world with their wonderful imagination. —N.B.

Text copyright © 2016 by Linda Glaser
Illustrations copyright © 2016 by Lerner Publishing Group, Inc.

KAR-BEN PUBLISHING
A division of Lerner Publishing Group, Inc.
241 First Avenue North
Minneapolis, MN 55401 USA
1-800-4-KARBEN

Website address: www.karben.com

Main body text set in King George Light Clean. Typeface provided by Chank.

Library of Congress Cataloging-in-Publication Data

Glaser, Linda, author.
    On one foot / by Linda Glaser ; illustrated by Nuria Balaguer.
        pages cm
    Include's bibliographical references and index.
    Summary: "A young man travels to Jerusalem to learn the Torah. When he decides that the
greatest teacher will be able to teach him the entire Torah while standing on one foot, he gets
laughed at and shooed away. Finally, he meets the great Rabbi Hillel, who is willing to help
him"— Provided by publisher.
    ISBN 978-1-4677-7842-8 (lb : alk. paper) —
    ISBN 978-1-4677-7847-3 (pb : alk. paper) —
    ISBN 978-1-4677-9608-8 (eb pdf)
    1. Hillel, active 1st century B.C.-1st century A.D—Juvenile fiction.
[1. Beth Hillel and Beth Shammai—Juvenile fiction.]
I. Balaguer, Nuria, illustrator. II. Title.
PZ7.G48047On 2016
[Fic]—dc23   2015016342

Manufactured in the United States of America
1 – CG – 12/31/15

On One Foot

Linda Glaser

Illustrated by
Nuria Balaguer

KAR-BEN
PUBLISHING

Long ago, a somewhat foolish young man
traveled to the ancient city of Jerusalem to study.

"I want to learn the Torah," the young man said to himself.
"But I don't want just any teacher. I want a *great* teacher."

He sat under a tree on the outskirts of town and thought. "How will I figure out who is a truly great teacher?" He watched a bird perched on a nearby branch standing on one foot.

"What a clever bird," he thought, "to stand on one foot and not topple over."

"That's it!" He jumped up. "A great teacher would be clever enough to stand on one foot." His eyes widened at the thought. "In fact, a truly great teacher could teach me the whole Torah while standing on one foot."

So off he went to search in the
bustling city of Jerusalem.

Soon, he came upon a rabbi who was busy studying. **"Hello, Rabbi,"** he said. **"Can you teach me the whole Torah while standing on one foot?"**

"Ha!" laughed the rabbi. **"Do you know how many books there are in the Torah? There are five."** He held up five fingers. **"Do you really think I can teach you all that while standing on one foot? Ha! Not even the great Rabbi Hillel could do that!"** He fell on the ground laughing.

The young man stamped his foot. **"Stop laughing at me!"** But the rabbi continued to laugh. The young man kicked angrily at a clod of dirt and stomped away.

Soon he came upon another rabbi. **"Rabbi, can you teach me the whole Torah while standing on one foot?"**

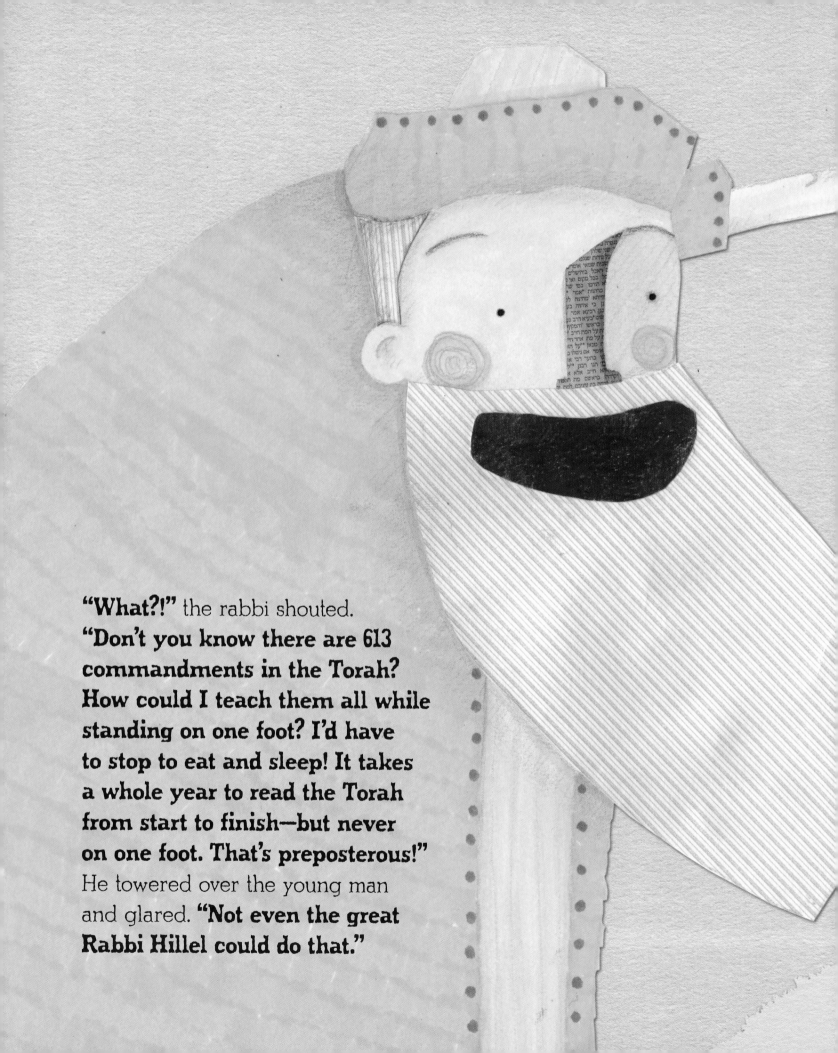

"**What?!**" the rabbi shouted. "**Don't you know there are 613 commandments in the Torah? How could I teach them all while standing on one foot? I'd have to stop to eat and sleep! It takes a whole year to read the Torah from start to finish—but never on one foot. That's preposterous!**" He towered over the young man and glared. "**Not even the great Rabbi Hillel could do that.**"

"Humph!" The young man stormed off, all hot in the face. Finding a great teacher was not going to be easy.

He trudged through the streets scowling at every person he saw. And they all scowled right back at him.

Soon he came upon the famous Rabbi Shammai and asked him, **"Rabbi, can you teach me the whole Torah while standing on one foot?"**

Rabbi Shammai scowled. **"Don't insult me with such a silly question. Not even Rabbi Hillel would tolerate it. Now go!"** he shouted, shaking his fist.

The young man could hardly get away fast enough. By now he feared he would never find a teacher. "Did I come all this way for nothing?" he asked himself.

The sun was setting as he came upon a group of children playing in the square. **"Get out of my way!"** he snapped.

"What's your hurry? We were only playing," one of the children said in surprise. But they all moved to let him pass.

The young man strode by, still scowling.

"Where are you going?" another called out.

"Can we help?" asked a third.

The young man turned back and blinked in surprise. No one had offered to help him all day.

"I am looking for a great rabbi who can teach me the whole Torah while standing on one foot," he told the children.

"Oh, let's try that!" They all giggled. **"What fun!"** They each stood on one foot and recited as fast as they could. But soon they all toppled to the ground laughing.

"We can't do it. You should go to Rabbi Hillel."
They pointed the way. "If anyone can do it, he
can. He's the wisest rabbi in all of Jerusalem.
And he's also the kindest."

So off the young man went.

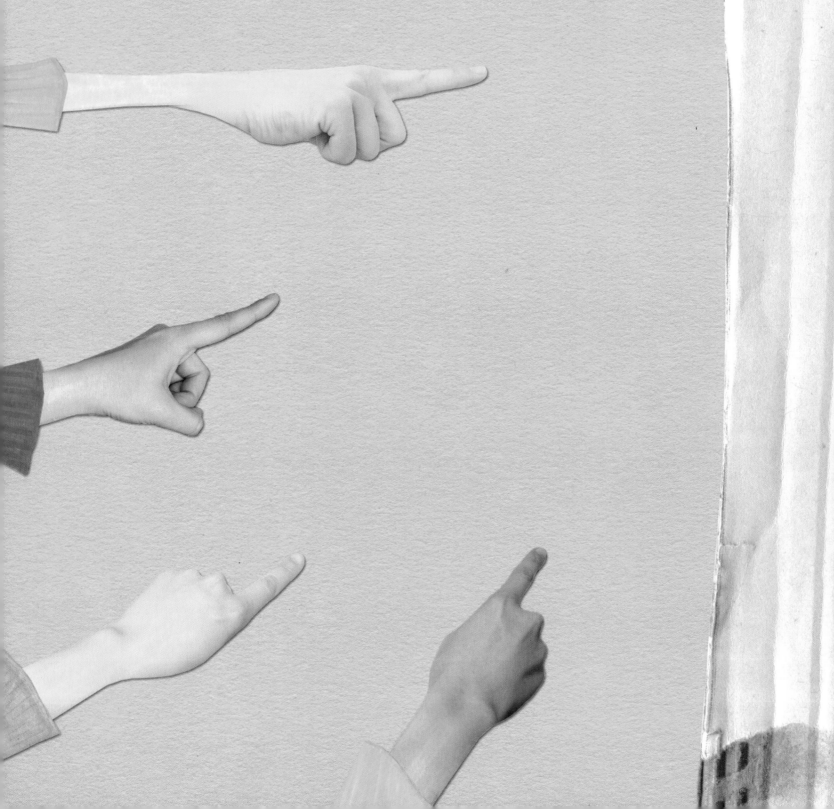

Meanwhile, the kind, gentle Rabbi Hillel was spending his day teaching people who came to him with questions. He listened carefully to each one and gave each a thoughtful response. "So many questions," thought Rabbi Hillel. "So much to learn."

At that moment, he heard a knock on the door. **"Please come in!"** he called—even though it was already growing dark.

The young man entered. **"Oh, Rabbi Hillel, can you teach me the whole Torah while standing on one foot?"**

The rabbi looked at him. The young man held his breath. What would the great rabbi do?

Rabbi Hillel did not fall on the ground laughing or shout "Preposterous!" or shake his fist at him. He did not stand on one foot either.

Instead, he waited patiently to make sure the young man was listening. Then he calmly spoke. ***"Do not do to others what you do not want them to do to you."***

"**What?**" said the young man.
"**Is that the whole Torah?**"

Rabbi Hillel nodded. "**The rest is just comments and explanations.**"

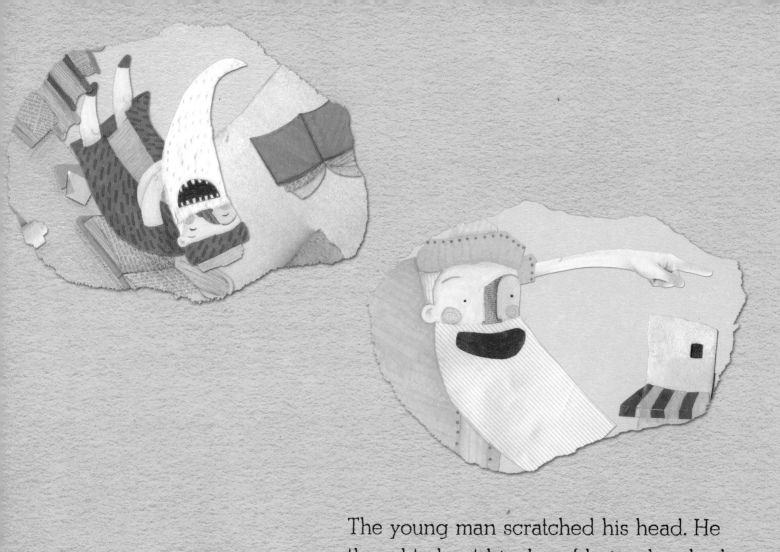

The young man scratched his head. He thought about his day of being laughed at and insulted. He thought of how he'd scowled at strangers and how they'd scowled back.

He scratched his head. **"I don't like to be insulted or scowled at. So I shouldn't do that to other people?"**

"I think that would be a good way to live," said Rabbi Hillel gently.

"Hmmm, I'd like to try it," said the not-so-foolish young man.

"Good," said Rabbi Hillel. "Come, my student. Let's go study."

Rabbi Hillel's wise words spread far and wide, from one person to the next . . . and from one generation to the next . . . all the way down to us.

Do not do to others what you do not want them to do to you.

Words that are wise enough to last a lifetime . . .

And yet simple enough
to say while standing on
one foot.

Author's Note

Rabbi Hillel lived long ago. (Historians speculate around 110 BCE to 10 CE). Born in Babylon, he spent much of his life in Jerusalem studying and teaching Torah. Considered one of the great Jewish scholars, Rabbi Hillel was deeply wise and equally kind. He founded The House of Hillel, a school known for its gentle interpretation of Torah. Rabbi Hillel taught, **"Do not do to others what you do not want them to do to you."**

Other wise words attributed to Rabbi Hillel are:

"If am not for myself, who is for me?

And if I am only for myself, what am I?

And if not now, when?"